The Vanishing Pumpkin

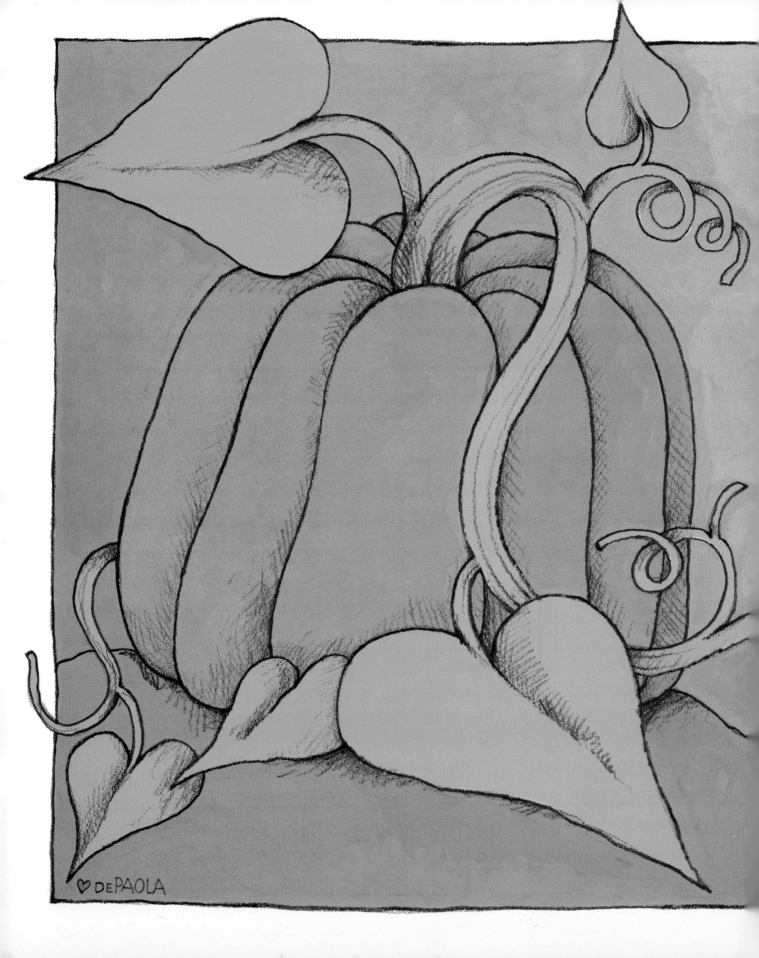

The Vanishing Pumpkin

by Tony Johnston
pictures by Tomie dePaola

G.P. Putnam's Sons
New York

For my favorite rapscallions,
Daddy and Ant Bon

Title name created by
Jennifer Johnston

Text copyright © 1983 by Tony Johnston
Illustrations copyright © 1983 by Tomie dePaola

Library of Congress Cataloging in Publication Data
Johnston, Tony.
The vanishing pumpkin.
Summary: A 700-year-old woman and an 800-year-old man,
both witches, go searching on Halloween night for the
pumpkin someone snitched from them.
/1. Halloween—Fiction. 2. Pumpkin—Fiction.
3. Witches—Fiction/I. dePaola, Tomie, ill. II. Title.
PZ7.J6478Van 1983 /E/ 83-3122
ISBN 0-399-20991-3
ISBN 0-399-20992-1 (pbk.)
Second impression

There was a 700-year-old woman. There was an 800-year-old man. They were rocking by the fire as the sun came up.

"Old man," said the old woman. "That sun reminds me of something."

"What?" asked the old man.

"Pumpkins. And pumpkins remind me of Halloween. And that's what day it is."

"Lucky lizards!" croaked the old man. "Fetch the
pumpkin we've been saving, and let's make a pumpkin
pie."

The old woman would have done that, but the pumpkin had vanished from sight.

She looked in the coffeepot.
No pumpkin.

She looked in the bed.
No pumpkin.

She looked in her purse of magic powders.
No pumpkin. Not a single one.

"Snitched!" she cried in a 700-year-old voice. "Our Halloween pumpkin's been snitched!"

"Great snakes!" croaked the old man. "Who would dare snitch a pumpkin from an 800-year-old man?"

And they set off down the road.

They went as fast as a 700-year-old woman and an 800-year-old man can. In fact, they fairly flew.

They met a ghoul perched on a fence post.
The old man flew up and hollered out, "Ghoul, where is it?"

"Dunno," growled the ghoul.
And he didn't. He didn't even know what *it* was.
"Tell him what it is," suggested the old woman.
"Our pumpkin," hollered the old man. "Where is it?"
"Dunno," growled the ghoul.
And he began to search for the pumpkin.

He looked underneath himself.　　　He looked behind himself.

He looked behind the old woman. He looked behind the old man.

"Stop that," cried the old man, "or I'll do you such a trick!"
"Please do," growled the ghoul.

So the old man made him thin as an onionskin. And he peered right through him, hoping to find the pumpkin hidden in a sneaky place.

The old woman clapped.

The ghoul clapped.

Even the old man clapped at that trick.

But they did not find the pumpkin. So the old man made him a normal ghoul again.

"Oh, where is that pumpkin?" croaked the old man. "I want my pumpkin pie."

So they set off down the road.

They went as fast as a 700-year-old woman and an 800-year-old man can. In fact, they fairly flew.

The ghoul came right behind. He wanted to see more tricks. (He wanted some pumpkin pie too.)

They met a rapscallion picking mushrooms.

The old man flew up and hollered out, "Rapscallion, where's the —, the —, the —"

"Pumpkin," whispered the old woman.

"Exactly," muttered the old man. "Where is it?"

The rapscallion thought about that.
He looked behind a rock.
No pumpkin.

He looked under his feet
(which was hard to do).
No pumpkin.

He looked in his mushroom basket. No pumpkin.

"Will a mushroom do?" he asked.

"Never!" shouted the old man. "I shan't eat mushroom pie. It's pumpkin pie or nothing!"

"Then it's nothing," said the rapscallion, grinning.

"Rapscallion, don't be fresh with an 800-year-old man," snapped the old man, "or I'll do you such a trick!"

"Please do," said the rapscallion, grinning.

So the old man turned him upside down, there be-
tween earth and sky, to shake that pumpkin out.
  The old woman clapped. The ghoul clapped. The
rapscallion clapped. Even the old man clapped at that
fine trick.

But not one single pumpkin fell from the rapscallion.
So the old man put him down again.

   "Oh, where is that pumpkin?" croaked the old man. "I
want my pumpkin pie."

   So they set off down the road.

They went as fast as a 700-year-old woman and an 800-year-old man can. In fact, they fairly flew.
The ghoul and the rapscallion came right behind.

They wanted to see more tricks.
(They wanted some pumpkin pie too.)
They met a varmint right then and there.

The old man flew up and bawled out, "Varmint, did
you see a pumpkin go by? A big fat one?"

"A great big fat one?" asked the varmint.

"Yes! Yes!" cried the old man, jumping up and down.

"Nope," said the varmint. And he laughed wickedly.

"Wicked! Wicked! Wicked!" shouted the old man. "I'll
do you such a trick for tricking me!"

"Please do," laughed the varmint.

So the old man turned him into a black cat and gave him lots of fleas.

The old woman clapped. The ghoul clapped. The rapscallion clapped. The old man clapped at his own trick. The varmint scratched. But no matter how he scratched, he never scratched a pumpkin.

So the old man brought him back again.

"Oh, where is that pumpkin?" croaked the old man. "I want my pumpkin pie."

So they set off down the road.

They went as fast as a 700-year-old woman and an 800-year-old man can. In fact, they fairly flew.

The ghoul and the rapscallion and the varmint came

right behind. They wanted to see more tricks. (They wanted some pumpkin pie too.)

They met a 900-year-old wizard, rocking by a fire as the sun went down.

The old man flew up. And he saw that it was no fire at all. It was—the pumpkin, carved into a jack-o'-lantern and grinning from ear to ear!

The old man felt like yelling. But you don't yell at a 900-year-old wizard. (He might turn you into a lizard.)

"I borrowed your pumpkin," said the wizard.

"Snitched," muttered the old man.

"*Borrowed.* For my jack-o'-lantern. Nothing but the best for me."

"Great grizzlies!" moaned the old man. "I'll never have my pumpkin pie."

"Pie," said the wizard. "That reminds me of something."

"What?" asked the old woman.
"Pie reminds me of pie. And when I finished my jack-o'-lantern, that's what I made for you."
"WHERE?" the old man asked.

"Oh, dear," said the wizard. "It was just here." And he began to search for the pumpkin pie.

He looked inside the jack-o'-lantern. No pie. He looked under his beard. No pie. He looked under his hat. And—there it was (along with a bat).

So they all sat down and gobbled it up.
Now what do you think of that?